ISBN 978-1-334-11632-2
PIBN 10748798

1 MONTH OF
FREE
READING

at

www.ForgottenBooks.com

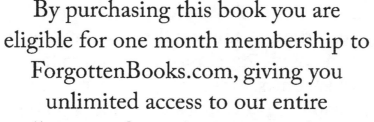

By purchasing this book you are eligible for one month membership to ForgottenBooks.com, giving you unlimited access to our entire collection of over 1,000,000 titles via our web site and mobile apps.

To claim your free month visit:

www.forgottenbooks.com/free748798

English
Français
Deutsche
Italiano
Español
Português

www.forgottenbooks.com

Mythology Photography **Fiction**
Fishing Christianity **Art** Cooking
Essays Buddhism Freemasonry
Medicine **Biology** Music **Ancient
Egypt** Evolution Carpentry Physics
Dance Geology **Mathematics** Fitness
Shakespeare **Folklore** Yoga Marketing
Confidence Immortality Biographies
Poetry **Psychology** Witchcraft
Electronics Chemistry History **Law**
Accounting **Philosophy** Anthropology
Alchemy Drama Quantum Mechanics
Atheism Sexual Health **Ancient History**
Entrepreneurship Languages Sport
Paleontology Needlework Islam
Metaphysics Investment Archaeology
Parenting Statistics Criminology
Motivational

The Eagle

(RUPERT'S LAND COLLEGE MAGAZINE)

VOL. II   MAY 1930

The Desire
for Better Things

is readily gratified by the visitor to Dingwall's, where the atmosphere of distinctiveness prevails.

"Distinctiveness" is the keynote of the choice collections of skilfully designed jewellery, which reflects the latest and most exclusive designs from Paris and London.

The charm of individuality in the Gift of Delight is always assured if selected at

Dingwall's

Western Canada's Finest Jewellery Store

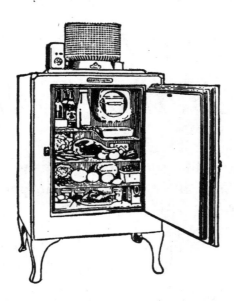

DEDICATED TO THE PARENTS

Miss Cynthia Dare was the brightest of all
  The pupils who studied at college.
She danced through her lessons while others would crawl;
  The girls were amazed at her knowledge.
But not so her parents! Just ask them, for they know,
  They'd answer, "Mens sana in corpore sano."

A body that's healthy, a mind that is clear,
  These two you will find go together.
Such pupils will thrive ev'ry month in the year
  And youthful complaints they will weather.
Plain fare, always fresh, is the food for a scholar—
  On medical bills you'll save many a dollar.

"Make it safe to be hungry"

GENERAL ELECTRIC REFRIGERATORS

are demonstrated and sold exclusively by

55-59 PRINCESS ST.

Students' Luncheons

ARE

ALWAYS AVAILABLE

AT

Picardy's

ELEVEN STORES AT YOUR SERVICE

Pupils and Friends are respectfully requested to patronize our Advertisers

Rupert's Land College

Incorporated with St. John's College

122 CARLTON STREET, WINNIPEG

eee

Governing Body

The Governors and Board of St. John's College

Advisory Board

HIS GRACE, THE ARCHBISHOP OF RUPERT'S LAND (Chairman)
E. L. DREWRY, ESQ. (Vice-Chairman)
VEN. ARCHDEACON MCELHERAN
THE REV. G. A. WELLS, C.M.G.
D. A. CLARK, ESQ.
W. P. MOSS, ESQ.
J. A. MACHRAY, ESQ., K.C.

Ladies' Executive Board

MISS G. E. MILLARD, Chairman
MRS. S. P. MATHESON, Vice-Chairman
MRS. B. J. CURRY, Secretary
MRS. W. P. MOSS, Treasurer

MRS. J. E. BOTTERELL	MRS. W. CHANDLER
MRS. C. F. PENTLAND	MRS. GLENN FLORANCE
MRS. J. ADAMSON	MRS. GORDON CHOWN
MRS. H. D. MARTIN	MRS. J. H. RILEY

LADY TUPPER

Principal

MISS G. E. MILLARD

Editorial Staff

MISS PEARMAN

MISS JONES

RUTH WELLS

PHYLLIS WEBB

MISS SCHŒNAU

MISS SHORT

MARGARET BARTLETT

WINIFRED SPRINGETT

Form Representatives

JEAN MONCRIEFF

KATHARINE SAUNDERS

MARY KATE FLORANCE

BETTY POTTER

PATRICIA CHOWN

CONTENTS

	Page
Portrait of Miss Millard	4
Principal's Letter	5
Editorial Notes	6
Chronicle of Events	7
Behind the Scenes	8
The Hallowe'en Party	9
What We Saw of the Graduation Dance	10
A Dream	11
Impressions of the Gymnastic and Dancing Display	11
A Dream	12
The Mongrel's Perfection	13
Boarding School Notes	14
Boarders' Handwork Class	15
Boarders' Literary Club	16
Boarders' Initiation, 1929	16
Boarders' Glee Singing	17
A Day Girl's Blue Monday	17
The Christmas Plays	18
The Game	20
The Snow Fairy — The Sleepy Lullaby — Ferns	21
Mission Notes	22
Highways	23
Anticipations of Our Trip to England	25
My Swing	25
Field Day	26
Getting Into Mischief	26
The Spirit of '30	27
These I Have Loved	28
Music	29
Sensations on First Donning Choir Robes	30
The House System	30
House Notes	31
Tokyo	38
The Sailor's Song — To a Horse	40
Sea-Gull	41
Something's Wrong!	41
Dawn	42
The French Club	42
Aquas Calientes	43
Sports	44
Team Criticisms	47
Form X Debate	48
I Looked Through the Brambles	49
The Magic Carpet	49
Footsteps	50
Art Notes	53
The Studio Tea	54
Great Expectations	54
Sailing	55
The Needle and Thread	55
Kindergarten Notes	56
Courage	57
The Fight of the Braves	57
The Guide Movement at Rupert's Land	58
Forms II and III	58
Head Girls	59
Ye Elevens of 1928-29	60
Old Girls' News	62

MISS G. E. MILLARD

The Eagle

Vol. II.   MAY 1930.   No. 1.

PRINCIPAL'S LETTER

Rupert's Land College,
Winnipeg, Easter 1930.

Dear Girls,—

It seems a very short time ago that we were busily planning the first number of THE EAGLE, our bird which soared aloft once again after a rest of eight years!

Although the year has passed so quickly, a great deal has been accomplished; don't you agree?

First, and what I know has made our work and play much happier, is the complete renovation of the College. The cream walls, hardwood floors, and freshly-painted desks in the class-rooms; the attractive dining-hall; the comfortable, well-stocked library, and the charmingly-decorated bedrooms are the result of much time and thought on the part of our two College Boards. Owing to their careful planning, the work which took the whole Summer holiday, was completed and we were able to open school on the usual date. I should like to take this opportunity of extending to the Advisory Board and to the Ladies' Executive Board the appreciation of the whole School.

The formation of our four School Houses has been even more successful that I had dared to hope. The members of each House have worked with great enthusiasm to make their particular House worthy of the name it bears and the School of which it is a part. The various entertainments and teas that the Houses have given have not only helped to strengthen School Spirit, but have revealed much latent talent amongst the members.

Then I feel there has been a decided quickening in the Spirit of self-government. Girls in Senior Forms have been thinking much more seriously this year of the real meaning of self-government and have realized that unselfishness lies behind it. They have tried various experiments, and though they may not as yet be satisfied with the results, they may, I know, look forward to the future with confidence, realizing that though the growth of this spirit of unselfishness is slow, it is no less sure. Let us keep the ideal before us, believing that faith, co-operation and friendliness will some day accomplish that on which we have set our hearts—

. . . "A man's reach should exceed his grasp
Or what's a heaven for?"

Yours affectionately,

G. E. MILLARD.

5

EDITORIAL NOTES

THE EAGLE has, at any rate, had a longer life than its predecessor, for the last School Magazine issued came to an end at Volume I. In order to pay our bills we have had to accept donations from the proceeds of concerts, but when these notes appear in print our readers will have the satisfaction of knowing that all last year's debts have been paid.

As we have taken orders, and subscriptions, in advance this year there is every prospect of our meeting all expenses without any help from other funds. In that case it will be possible to organize the 1931 Magazine Committee in September, with the result that the girls of the School will have a still larger share in the production of their annual Magazine. It is probable that the standard of the articles will be raised and the labours of the Editorial Staff considerably lightened by beginning work in September.

It is a good idea for girls to save up the copies of the Magazine and to have them bound when they leave School. This record of their School life will prove most interesting to them in future years. A few copies of Volume I have been saved in case any girl wishes to complete her set for this purpose, but none will be available after the end of the Summer Term. These can be obtained from Miss Pearman for 25 cents.

It is disappointing that space will not allow us to include all the suitable material submitted in the Magazine; we hope that girls who have been unsuccessful this year will have better luck in future. In conclusion we should like to thank all those who have helped to make the Magazine a success by advertising, by writing articles, and by ordering copies.

SCHOOL CALENDAR 1929-1930

1929

Sept. 11—School reopened; welcome to Miss Chubb, Miss Johnson, Miss Loring, Miss Moss and Miss Pauli.

Sept. 20—Reception for parents and friends.

Oct. 2—Film of the first expedition to cross the Sahara.

Oct. 5—Film of "The Epic of the South Pole" at the Walker Theatre.

Oct. 12—Boarders' Picnic at River-Park. - Initiation of new Boarders.

Oct. 15—Field Day at Sargent Park.

Oct. 24—"The Only Way" (Martin Harvey Co.) at the Walker Theatre.

Oct. 25—Machray House Concert.

Oct. 29—Mrs. Carruthers gave a Tea for Rupert's Land Boarders.

Nov. 1—Commemoration Service at St. John's Cathedral.

Nov. 2—Hallowe'en Party.

Nov. 3—Twilight Organ Recital at St. Stephen's Church.

Nov. 7—"Hamlet" (Stratford-upon-Avon Co.) at the Walker Theatre.

Nov. 8—Mrs. Ernest Hare, of London, England, gave Senior Dancing Class a lesson in Greek dancing.

Nov. 9—"A Midsummer Night's Dream" at the Walker Theatre.

Nov. 10—Thanksgiving and half-term week-end.

Nov. 12—Maurice Colbourne spoke to the girls on "Bernard Shaw."

Nov. 13—"Arms and the Man" at the Walker Theatre.

Nov. 18—Miss Holden's talk on Indian Mission Work.

Nov. 19—Rupert's Land girls gave a display of Greek Dancing at the Junior Musical Club.

Nov. 29—Riverbend girls visited Rupert's Land for basketball match.

Dec. 2—English Folk Dances at the Walker Theatre.

Dec. 13—"Disraeli" film at the "Metropolitan."

Dec. 14—Basketball match, "Cubes" vs. Boarders. "Mother Goose" at the Walker Theatre.

Dec. 17 and 18—Christmas Plays in the School Assembly Hall.

Dec. 19—Kindergarten Christmas Party.

Dec. 20—School broke up for the Christmas holidays.

1930

Jan. 7—Boarders returned for Easter Term.
Jan. 8—School re-opened.
Jan. 20—Carleton Symphony Band at Walker Theatre.
Jan. 21—Some of the Seniors went to the Opening of Parliament.
Jan. 31—Eva L. Jones House Entertainment.
Feb. 7—Grade XI girls went to St. John's Dance.
Feb. 8—Boarders' "hike": Tea at Mrs. Claydon's.
Feb. 26—Rehearsal at the Walker Theatre.
Feb. 27—Gymnastic and Dancing Display at Walker Theatre.
Mar. 7—Winnipeg Skating Club Carnival.
Mar. 8—Hike in Kildonan Park: Tea at Mrs. Wells'.
Mar. 10—Prefects entertained the Staff.
Mar. 15—Boarders went to see film "The Taming of the Shrew."
Mar. 16—Boarders entertained by Miss Schœnau.
Mar. 17—Matheson House—St. Patrick's Tea.
Mar. 21—Basketball Match at Riverbend.
Mar. 27—Basketball Match, First and Second Teams.
Mar. 28—Basketball Match vs. Taché School.
Mar. 29—Basketball Match against Rupert's Land Old Girls.
April 4—Dalton House Entertainment.
April 11—End of Easter Term.
April 23—Beginning of Summer Term.
May 31—Grade X Dinner for Graduating Class.
June 13—Closing for the Summer holidays.
June 16—Departmental Examinations begin!!

FAITH STARKEY.

BEHIND THE SCENES

What was all this commotion? Girls in tunics everywhere. A voice from the wings, "We shall soon be starting." Whispers from the passages, "What time is it?—but *nobody* had a watch. Then a "Sh" from the stage, for the overture had started. Slowly and *silently* the girls found their partners and cried confusedly, "Which side is the platform?" Then up went the curtain, the familiar strains of a march started, and with smiling faces, and heads high, the girls made a *dignified* entrance. At last we knew—it was the annual display of gym and dancing by the girls of Rupert's Land College.

JEAN TOMLINSON.

THE HALLOWE'EN PARTY

The School once more had a most enjoyable Hallowe'en Party. A Sailors' Hornpipe (?), given by the skipper and crew of H.M.S. Rupert's Land, caused a considerable amount of amusement. Prizes were given for the prettiest and the most original costumes. Mary Lile Love won the former prize, while Betty Joyce and Frances Gilman were considered the most original couple in the room. Refreshments were served at the end of the evening and the smiling faces of all present were a sure proof that the party was successful.

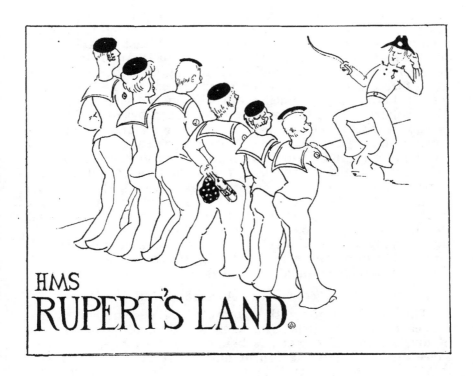

WHAT WE SAW OF THE GRADUATION DANCE, MAY 1929

The Statue in the Hall

The statue on the staircase gazed, we can but say it looked amazed. What has become of the old School, thus parting from the daily rule? Where were the tunics of dark blue? From whence came this most lovely view? Where were the stockings, long and black? There is a gown without a back! Why they are here in shivering groups, instead of hurrying, scurrying "Rups"? Who is this lovely thing in black? It's Miss Millard, alas! alack! Then I can see it is too true, the whole School has gone quite cuckoo. But here is our most brilliant Staff, that look prepared to laugh and laugh. Instead of sharply giving orders, they're beaming greetings to the Boarders, who have arrived all in a pucker; they have all donned best bib and tucker. This lovely group is going away —down to the dining-room, I'd say.

The Picture on the Dining-room Wall

The picture said within his heart, "The dining-room looks really smart." The rows of eagles, poised for flight, each on a name seem to invite you to, of a royal feast partake (oh! do forget the tummy-ache, that came upon the morning after, but think of all the fun and laughter, as all with grins upon their faces, madly hunted for their places). The feast proceeded, long and gay, until a lull was heard, we'll say; when Miss Millard got up to speak, none but the brave would dare to squeak their chairs or sneeze or cough aloud, to make a murmur in the crowd. Then Muriel, our trusty "Head," got up—what were those words she said? Then Jocelyn, as though she must, spouted at length of worms and dust; and Barbara Patterson must not be forgotten, as 'twas little she who prompted Terry to her feet to mutter words so strange but sweet. Then Nancy with great gusto rose, to say she felt she must propose a toast to Form Ten and their dinner (we'll say it really was a winner). And then all went upstairs, oh quite relieved of any cares that might have come to us with thoughts perchance of all successes of our dance.

Queen Elizabeth on the Assembly Hall Wall

The hall is bright with colours gay, I wish it looked like this each day—the girls seem so excited, too, all in their gowns of lovely hue. The piano is being played by one, who with three others makes the fun of dancing to such merry tunes, in this room hung with bright balloons. Oh what is this unseemly noise? I'm sure it is those rowdy boys, who have arrived just now I see, from whence they came surprises me. Here's Mr. Burman and his guests—I hope my gown does

10

look its best.   After an hour or two of fun, they are retreating once again—down to the dining-room to sup, I do hope that their time's not up.   It was such fun to watch them all, I wish that I were at the ball.   But here they come a half hour after, all sparkling gay with fun and laughter, to have a few short moments play before it's time to go away.   Goodbyes and thankyous quickly said, they all go home "and so to bed." (?????)

B. KELLY.

A DREAM

One day I fell asleeping,
  I dreamt a dream so grand,
I lived with lots of other girls
  In happy Rupert's Land.

The days were short and happy,
  My heart with joy was full;
I thought myself a lucky girl
  To live in such a School.

The teachers they were lovely,
  The School was surely blest
With Miss Millard, Miss Jones, Miss Short,
  Miss Moss and all the rest.

But then my dream grew very dark,
  I had to go away,
I couldn't bear to leave it all;
  I simply had to stay.

I moped and sighed, I sobbed and cried,
  My heart I nearly broke,
Till I rolled right off the sofa
  And from my dream awoke.

R. GLENNIE.
Age 9.

IMPRESSIONS OF THE GYMNASTIC AND DANCING. DISPLAY FROM THE AUDIENCE

The house was gradually filling up.   Girls in tunics were scurrying hither and thither, chatting and laughing gaily with friends in the audience.   Indeed, everybody seemed in the best of spirits.   Then the overture was played, the curtain raised, and on marched Rupert's Land College.   The march on was followed by a Senior and Junior Swedish Table, wands and free movements to music by the Midget Class.   Then came Intermediate and Senior skipping, parallels, combined apparatus, tactical marching, and horse, in which all classes took part.

The second part of the programme consisted of dancing. The wonderful technique showed careful training, and the artistic arrangement of "By the Sea" and "The Return of Persephone" was greatly commented upon. The enthusiastic reception of "Ten Little Nigger Boys," by the Baby Class, brought forth an encore.

The display was concluded by an effective lantern maze, and flowers were presented to Miss Welch in appreciation for her work throughout the year, and to Miss Pauli, whose accompaniment was greatly enjoyed.

The unanimous opinion was that the display had been in every way a success, giving great credit to Miss Welch and showing an unusual spirit of co-operation on the part of the pupils.

MURIEL HARTLEY.

_____

A DREAM

It must have been a dream—a bad dream. Nothing in real life could equal such a scene as was witnessed on the night of the twenty-seventh of February. The entire date in all its glory should be set down in full, for it is a memorable date in the history of our School—therefore we will set it down in all its glory—Thursday, February the twenty-seventh, of the year nineteen hundred and thirty. On that night the Walker Theatre swarmed with violently excited pupils of Rupert's Land, all taking vastly important parts in the Annual Gymnastic and Dancing Display, and all feeling, naturally, very nervous and decidedly hysterical.

Greatly inspired by the theatrical atmosphere of the narrow, dark passages and the little, brilliantly-lighted dressing rooms, groups of neatly garbed gymnasts sped lightly here and there uttering, at intervals, little shrieks and yells that quite outdid the valiant "Shushings" of those in command. Finally, at the appointed hour, two hundred "worn-out" girls presented themselves on the stage to take part in the march on, and to delight the eyes of fond parents and eager friends.

After these controlled efforts on the stage, the curtain, luckily a sound-proof curtain, descended, hiding from view the various antics of youth in the abandonment of delirious joy. Fresh make-up was applied by patient, controlled (?) people during the evening, until a final burst of energy of another kind quite swept those gentle people off their feet. What was it? They looked in amazement, to find themselves surrounded by dainty dancers in dress of airy pattern, who gradually glided onto the stage, allowing the startled appliers of cosmetics to collect their scattered wits and implements.

As the evening sped on, the atmosphere became a little calmer, but nevertheless remained of an excited nature. Groups of weary people were seen supporting the stone walls of the theatre, while smaller members, who had not been borne homeward by relations, frankly slept until they were prodded into wakefulness by the sound of a muffled clapping. Could those have been the familiar strains of our National Anthem? Could Miss Welch have received her flowers already? Could it be possible that the Gym Display was over? It could be possible; it was possible. The supporters of the stone walls of the theatre slowly got into a convenient position for walking, the muffled roar became an unmuffled reality, and sleeping people soon found it safer to be in motion, or in a less densely populated spot.

The next day we read that a most successful display had been put on by the members of Rupert's Land College. After careful consideration we learnt that we had been present on that occasion and that it wasn't a dream, but an event.

R. W.

THE MONGREL'S PERFECTION

Out in the cold, wide world
　　All alone.
In the oozy, black bogs he curled
　　With a bone
　　And dreamt.

There was a fire burning bright
Over my head quite late at night,
On, on I slept,
My bone I kept,
Then up I got
Upstairs to trot,
On to the bed
With a clean white spread
The pillow on which I lay my head,
And lick the face of a master young
With a red and cool and cultured tongue.
In the soft grey dawn he 'roused me,
And, after his hot, refreshing tea,
We dwindled off for a hunt.

BETTY SNELL.
Age 15.

13

BOARDING SCHOOL NOTES

The Boarders—Seniors, Juniors and "Little Ones"—have enjoyed a happy year, with many and varied activities. On our return in September we were delighted with the brightness and colour of our newly decorated School. We thank Mrs. Moss and all who devoted so much thought and time during the Summer to making each room beautiful and individual. The happy possessors of "Windflower Room" rejoice in their dark furniture, a contrast to the cream of "Marigold," the green of "Spring Gardens," and the mauve of "Orchid." The Cubicles' too—blue, mauve, gold and rose—are a delight. But most of all we love the dining-room. Its buff walls, brightened

A BOARDERS' PICNIC

by the gay orange fruit in the curtains, the rich blue of furniture, chairs and tables, the latter laid with cream lace mats, and decorated with orange bowls of Autumn leaves or flowers— who could fail to enjoy a meal in such a sunshiny room?

It was decided this year to introduce into the Boarding School the Prefect System which has been so successful in the Day School, so Leona McLaughlin and Faith Starkey were appointed Senior Prefects, and Bernice Patterson and Judy Moss Junior Prefects. These girls have shown by their steady influence, loyalty and common-sense that the Prefect system is a great help to the School, and we congratulate them on their success.

This year we have enjoyed an unusual number of theatre parties, including "The Only Way," "Hamlet," "Arms and the Man," "Disraeli," "Morris Dances," "The Pirates of Penzance," "R. U. R.," and the wonderful film of Scott's expedition to the Antarctic.

Tea Parties on Sunday afternoons have been much enjoyed, a special occasion being the time when Miss Schœnau entertained us in her suite in Devon Court, when chatter, good things to eat, and the gramophone made the time pass all too quickly. There have been some gay supper parties in Miss Holditch's room, when we sat round on the floor, toasted sandwiches, and Miss Millard in the room below wondered what all the laughter and noise was about.

Then one day the "Cubes" were invited in a long rhymed invitation to Tea with Miss Bannister—but not unless we answered in verse—so for a few days brains ticked. Then the day arrived. We all came in from a hike, some hot, some cold, all ready to relax, and there awaiting us was . . . oooohh! cakes, sandwiches, cookies, candies, ice cream, nuts and tea, green tables, cushions, doylies, comfies. There we sat one hour, two hours, three hours, while the others peeked in the keyhole and sniffed enviously "outside" the barred door.

Extra shopping parties arranged by our "School Mothers" at Christmas were much appreciated, as also the interest they take in us throughout the year. Miss Pearman's Tea Parties, when each "daughter" is privileged to bring a guest, are much enjoyed.

The In-week-ends have again been a feature of Boarding School life. The Autumn picnic to River Park, when we ate hot dogs, climbed trees, and did gymnastic stunts, was followed in the Winter by hikes to St. Vital and Kildonan. Whether on skis, snowshoes, or merely in moccasins, we enjoyed the exhilarating air and fun outdoors. Our hearty thanks are tendered to Mrs. Wells and Mrs. Claydon for so kindly entertaining our big family to Tea on these occasions. Mrs. Carruthers is another of the kind friends who thought of the Boarders and gave a Tea specially for them in October.

The Initiation Ceremony on the first in-week-end, and impromptu concerts on other occasions, in which many girls have shown initiative and ability, have entertained us on Saturday evenings. So in-week-ends give many opportunities for community outings and entertainment.

BOARDERS' HANDWORK CLASS

The Boarders have their handwork class again this year, but instead of the grumbling over the prospect of sewing on blue flannel kimonas, everyone looks forward to the Monday evenings spent in the Studio under Miss Short's supervision. We started the year with batik dyeing, and many stockings, dresses and even shoes changed colour during the process. Scarves were the only thing attempted, and as far as originality is concerned they were certainly a success. Raffia work was done by many of the girls and colourful and artistic mats were the result. At present half the class is working on bright-coloured homespun, with yarn, which eventually will become pillow tops. The other half are filling the Studio with "spirits," by dyeing various patterns on leather and making many useful things.

We all feel very grateful to Miss Short for teaching us so many interesting occupations, which have certainly made our class a success.

BOARDERS' LITERARY CLUB

Senior and Junior groups of the Club have met every week.

Among the authors we have read are Barrie, De la Mare, Masefield, W. H. Drummond, Thornton Wilder, Galsworthy and Hardy. One-act plays of to-day and some short stories have also been read.

We debated as to whether examinations justify their existence, Ruth Wells and Faith Starkey being protagonists. The motion against examinations was carried 7 to 4, despite good defence by the opposers.

The Junior group has enjoyed reading Grahame's "Wind in the Willows" and Maeterlinck's "Bluebird."

BOARDERS' INITIATION, 1929

We were awakened with the orders from the Boarding School Old Girls, and had to obey them all day long. We made their beds, ran messages, and did everything that they could think of making us do. Then, worn out after the picnic, we got home to find a sweet little message on each bureau: "Part your hair in the middle to-night." Oh dear! we all looked terrible of course, and when we reached the dining-room we found nothing but spoons to eat with. Luckily the meat was tender, but alas, even Mrs. Fenton planned against us, and we had lovely runny tapioca for dessert. Forks alone proved helpful in eating the latter! After prayers we were calmly told we were to amuse the Old Girls for the evening. We tried every way for revenge, and so we used the Boarders' clothes for costumes. We were asked to produce the play of Cinderella with but twenty minutes' preparation. Ambition was shown by some, as for instance making an effort to get ready for the walk in winter—and it just took the victim twenty minutes to do it! It was very funny, and in the end, in the dark, we all swore to be true R.L.C. Boarders.

Much-needed nourishment was served afterwards in the sitting-room and the new girls were then waited upon—we went to bed well satisfied in more ways than one.

BOARDERS' GLEE SINGING

The glee singing last term took place one evening a week for half an hour, during which the Boarders would exercise their vocal organs by singing such numbers as "Annie Laurie," "Comin' Thro' the Rye," "John Peel," and other favorite songs. Owing to the examinations ahead, and having naturally less spare time, at any rate for the Senior Boarders, we have dropped the weekly "warbling" until next winter term, when we hope to resume not only in "unison," but "part" singing.

M. H. P.

A DAY GIRL'S BLUE MONDAY

You are unmercifully awakened at a quarter to seven and told it is "time to get up." You drag your weary bones out of bed and shut the window. Before breakfast you either practise or do homework for about an hour. While at breakfast one of your heartless family hints that you must have got dressed in a hurry, as you have no tie on and there are cat's hairs all over your tunic, not to mention a rip in the sleeve of your blouse. As soon as you are finished you rush upstairs to put on your tie, and find a hole in the heel of your stocking. You hastily darn it, then run for your books, coat and hat. On arriving at the garage you find that your father can't get the car started and wants you to get in and push this and poke that and pull the other while he cranks it. You finally get started and arrive at school at ten past nine, feeling as if you had already done a good day's work. When asked why you were late, you give the oft repeated excuse, "Dad drove me down."

At recess, after being caught once on the upper corridor and twice on the lower, you finally manage to get an order mark.

You rush home at noon with a French book under one arm, intending to study for a test to be given that afternoon. But alas for good resolutions! You don't open the book.

In the afternoon you manage to get yourself into trouble again by aiming a crunched-up piece of paper at a friend and hitting a teacher. For this you receive a conduct mark!

At half past three you gather up your books and go home. From then until the time you go to bed you study and practise without intermission except for dinner. When you finally

17

climb into bed it is only to dream of school troubles and a jumble of the three R's. A seeming five minutes later you are again awakened by an irate parent informing you that you have been called three times already. "How do you expect to get to school on time?"

M. WALSTON.
F. GOWAN.
K. MATHEWS.

THE CHRISTMAS PLAYS

This year, the usual Christmas play was replaced by three one-act plays that were chosen for their variety of ideas. Three members of the Staff undertook the task of training a hundred or more eager "actresses," and their results were witnessed by all the parents and friends on December 19th.

"A Christmas Party" — produced by Miss Pearman — was the first, in which all the leading parts were played by members of the Kindergarten and other Junior Forms. The entrance of Santa Claus, and the eagerness of the little ones on receiving their gifts, put everyone in a jovial mood.

"The Spring Green Lady"—a fantasy, produced by Miss Bannister—was received with equal pleasure, and the leading characters—Dorothy Withers, the Captive Princess, and Jean Wells, the Wandering Minstrel, sang with almost professional feeling, if not ease!

"The Land of Heart's Desire"—produced by Miss Jones and Miss Short—was a story of Irish folk-lore, in which a half-fairy child is wooed away into the heart of the forest by a wood-sprite despite the efforts of her parents and a wandering priest. Sheila Campbell as the Fairy Child, Judy Moss as the Wood Sprite, and Eleanor Lodge as Priest, played the principal parts with spirit, but we must confess that very important parts were being played behind scenes. Phyllis Webb, the "ghostly green glimmer in the trees," was aided in this role by a trusty green torch, while members of the Choral Society and Miss Pauli provided music that was most mysterious and supernatural!

The plays were most successful, and the different types prevented the entertainment from seeming too long.

R. W.

PROGRAMME I.

"A CHRISTMAS PARTY"
By Ragna B. Eskit

Eileen..E. Chandler
Ann...A. Campbell
God Mother...M. K. Florance
Mary...B. Potter
Jack..H. Hutchinson
Jill...B. Parker
Old Mother Hubbard...M. Bedford
Jack Horner...P. Moorhouse
Miss Muffett..P. Chown
Bo-Peep...V. Bannerman
Boy Blue..J. Gray
Queen of Hearts...B. Trimmer
Knave of Hearts...B. Strang
Jack of the Beanstalk...M. Dennison
Red Riding Hood..E. Mitten
Cinderella..M. L. Love
Prince..E. Henderson
Old King Cole..D. Lawson
Santa Claus...M. Dorset
Three Fiddlers.............................M. Chisholm, R. Glennie, E. Rogers,
Christmas Goblins...............................R. Heppner. G. Johnson, S. Lear, P. Parrish, S. Roberts,
B. South, M. Tomkins, C. Wardrope, M. Gale White

Accompanist...M. H. Pauli
Costumes...The Mothers
Producer ....M. Pearman

PROGRAMME II.

"THE SPRING GREEN LADY"
Adapted from the Phantasy "Martin Pippin in the Apple Orchard"
by Eleanor Farjeon
Produced by G. Bannister

Wandering Minstrel...Jean Wells
Emperor's Daughter................................Dorothy Withers

SCENE I.—An Orchard.

Yvonne Wells	Shirley Jackson	Cristine Machray
Roberta Yates	Olive French	Joan Reynolds

SCENE II.—Same.

Jean Shave	Dorothy Donovan	Bernice Patterson
Nora Whitley	Kathleen Hopps	Betty Snell

SCENE III.—Same.

Mary Walston	Margaret White	Winifred Walker
Ruth Fletcher	Betty Tisdale	Marguerite Hayes

Costumes..V. Short
Dances...G. Bannister
Accompanist...G. Bannister
Music...Ballet Music from Faust

PROGRAMME III.

"THE LAND OF HEART'S DESIRE"
By W. B. Yeats

Maurteen Bruin...Marjorie Hunt
Bridget Bruin..Viola Glennie
Shawn Bruin..Elizabeth Campbell
Mary Bruin...Sheila Campbell
Father Hart...Eleanor Lodge
A Fairy Child...Judy Moss

The scene is laid in the Barony of Kilmacowen, in the County of Sligo, and at a remote time.

Produced by.............................V. Short and G. Jones
Music...M. Pauli

Spinning Wheel kindly lent by W. H. McPherson, Esq.

THE GAME

Oh! our Rupert's Land is known from east to west.
O'er all the wide prairies its name is the best.
And save for short tunics we blemish have none,
We seek for the heights, and we seek not alone.
So ready at all times with a helpful hand,
There never was school like our loved Rupert's Land.

We stayed not for supper, we rushed from our home,
We walked the whole distance where street-car was none.
But ere we alighted at Rupert's Land gate
The captains had tossed, and we wriggled in, late.
For a daring young team, who played well at their worst,
Sought to shatter the pride of our basketball "First."

So boldly they entered the Assembly Hall,
Fast staring eyes, whisperings, cheering and all,
Then spake our brave captain, her hand on her hip,
While the other young maid curled a haughty red lip,
"Oh, come ye in peace here, or come ye in war,
Or to play basketball on our nice shiny floor?"

"I long wooed your forwards—my suit they denied—
Love swells like the Solway but ebbs like its tide.
And now am I come with this good team of mine
To gain but one basket (or two would be fine).
There are teams in this city more worthy by far
Who would willingly play when they knew who we are."

The coach blew the whistle—their side won the toss—
But the funny part was that their captain seemed cross.
She looked down to blush and she looked up to sigh
With a pout on her lip and a gleam in her eye.
Phil Webb pressed her hand ere her tears could fall far,
"I wish we'd begin," said Margaret to Norah.

So quick in their passing, so eager of face,
That never a match such perfection did grace.
While our captain did fret and their captain did fume,
And the flustered coach blew on the whistle too soon,
And the other team whispered, " 'Twere better by far
To have matched our fair cousin with Audrey Gar."

One jump at our forward, one shout in her ear,
One more basket to win, and time up drawing near.
So light to the basket the brown ball she swung,
So lightly behind it the fair maiden sprung.
"It's won!" Over legs, floor, and benches we flit.
"We've refreshments to follow," quoth our Mary Whit.

S. CAMPBELL.

THE SNOW FAIRY

I am the Snow Fairy,
I am glittery and glary.
I play with the children all day,
We have the greatest fun at play.

I come from the sky
And I never, never cry.
I have goldy wings,
They are the very best of things.

J. STEPHENS.
Age 7.

THE SLEEPY LULLABY

Sleep, baby dear,
Close your eyes of blue,
Here comes the Sandman,
He has a dream for you.
Shall it be a bluebird
Wrapped in a rosebud?
The sleepy Sandman I have heard,
So sleep my baby darling.

P. CHOWN.
Age 8.

FERNS

Like lovely lace,
Like a lovely face,
Like a graceful lady,
Like a cradle and a baby.

Waving in the fields,
Beside the corn that yields,
Above, the blue, blue sky,
Above, the birds that fly.

C. PENTLAND.
Age 9.

MISSION NOTES

The Hay River **Mission.** The Hay River Mission School at Great Slave Lake educates fifty Indian and Esquimo boys and girls, many of whom come long distances to enrol. Besides supporting two girls, we send Christmas presents to each pupil. Our hearty thanks are due to Mr. and Mrs. C. B. Montgomery for their help in choosing and dispatching these gifts by freight. In a letter of thanks, Miss Neville, the Matron-in-Charge, writes, "They are lovely toys; we have had so much pleasure going through them. The children are getting very excited; being so kindly remembered each year they know what they have to look forward to. The decorations that were with them are so acceptable, and the artificial flowers. For a long time we have been wishing for something for the Church at Easter, so the white flowers are put away for that."

The Garden Party in June, when we raised the support of our two girls, was a great success. Racing on the lawn, Aunt Sally, Hoop-la, a mysterious "Swimming Match," and an orchestra for the Tea Dance provided entertainment. The charming tea tables, ice cream booth, candy and home-made cooking stalls were well patronized, while the fancy stall and doll stall contributed handsomely to the total sum raised.

The Zenana Bible and Medical Mission. For years we have supported Nanu Kissan, an orphan Indian girl, at the Mission School at Manmad. She has now finished school and is training for her life work. She writes a very creditable letter in English—to her a foreign language—as the following extract from one lately received shows: "Very many salaams to you. . . . I am working now. Also I am taking the Bible training too. Sometimes at our examinations we have to give a lesson to the little girls. I am trying hard. Thank you so much for the present you so kindly sent to me. I like it very much."

We also sent a contribution of $90 towards Dr. Lambert's salary. Our interest in the hospital work was much stimulated by a visit while on furlough from Miss Holden, a Toronto graduate, who is nursing at the Canadian hospital at Nasik under Dr. Lambert. She brought with her dolls, dressed in Indian costumes by the patients, which she used to illustrate her descriptions of the life of women and girls in India. We hope to adopt a bed in the new wing of the hospital and name it "The Rupert's Land Cot."

The Annual Tea and Gift Shop in November was a great success, each House contributing its share to the total of $135.46 raised during the afternoon.

Christmas Bales. This year again each Form provided clothes, toys, and a Christmas dinner for a poor family at Christmas. Letters of thanks received tell of the happiness these bales of good things bring to homes where a visit from Santa Claus is often unexpected.

C. M. HOLDITCH.

HIGHWAYS

The old trail had been used by the buffaloes year after year in their migrations, across the plain, down in the valley and up onto the higher plateau, but always within close range of the river's course.

This year was different though. Strange two-legged creatures, clothed in the fur skins of animals and decorated with gay feathered head-dress, had swooped down upon their haunt and driven them away. No longer could the buffalo follow their old trail along the river or graze on the grassy banks, or wade in the cooling waters.

Then the Indians, who had driven away the buffalo, began to use the river banks as a trail of theirs, for in most places the waters were too treacherous for their frail canoes. Each Spring they would go down the trail laden with skins and hides from the North; in the Fall they would return gaily bedecked with bright beads and trinkets and behaving very wildly, even for them, firing off their guns and rifles which they obtained from the white men of the East in exchange for the skins.

After awhile some of these white men came along the trail with the Indians, and soon many white soldiers passed along the river's bank. The white men returned but the Indians never again appeared. Soon the old trail became cut and rutted by wagon wheels. The white settlers came in covered wagons and camped on the river's bank. The few trees which grew there were chopped down and used for fire-wood.

More and more white men went along the old trail until at last a railroad was built nearby and great blustering steam engines rushed by at regular intervals. The old trail was paved with cement and became a modern highway with tourists in automobiles hurrying along over its surface and admiring the scenery as they go by.

Then from the blue sky above comes the sound of an airplane wending its way among the soft white clouds.

Thus the highway of the airplane and the highway of the old lumbering buffalo is the old river which flows on in a narrow ribbon unchanged by time.

JANE NICHOLLS.

Some of US to sea did go,
And some were left behind.

ELEANOR LODGE.
Age 14.

ANTICIPATIONS OF OUR TRIP TO ENGLAND

There will be so much to see and to do. The wonderful preparations, packing, shopping, etc. The excitement of catching the eastbound train; we shall probably be fussing for hours before train time! Then the sea, which as yet I have never seen, and the boat, the "Empress of Australia." The voyage, except for the possibility of a storm, seems a glorious prospect. We land at Southampton on July 9th, and proceed to Oxford by motor coach, via the New Forest. At Oxford we shall stay at Lady Margaret Hall. We shall also attend some lectures given by prominent people. Then we go to Stratford-upon-Avon, where we shall be billeted in small hotels and private homes. We shall make a special study of Shakespeare and attend nine Shakespearian plays. After this we shall go to London, and this I am looking forward to most of all. We are to see "all the sights," and are staying at Queen Alexandra's house near the Royal Albert Hall. Then we shall have a short time to visit relatives and friends before we depart again for good old Canada.

K. H. WICKENS.

MY SWING

I have a swing in the garden,
   And I swing on it oh! so high;
I can see old farmer Mardin
   As he cleans out his new pigsty.

I can see the old church steeple
   As it soars up into the sky,
And dozens and dozens of people,
   And the circus that stands so high.

I can see all the little brown huts
   As they stand in a long, straight row,
And the goat on the mountain that butts,
   While the people their grass do mow.

I can see right into the trees
   Where the robins build their nests,
And the dog who is gone in the knees
   And the cats that the people call pests.

JEAN ALEXANDER.
Age 11.

FIELD DAY
Broadcasted through "Alexander the Talking Car."

After a harum scarum ride, carrying two of the noble Staff, and none other than Miss Garland herself at the wheel, I charged through the gates of Sargent Park and was brought to a halt by the sudden use of my emergency brake. From my "ringside" seat I proceeded to gaze upon the wild antics of the girls of Rupert's Land College as they raced and chased, and bobbed and hopped, and leapt and jumped, for the athletic supremacy of the Houses. In a secluded corner of the old swimming pool, Miss Bartlett, Miss Webb and Miss Smith doled out "Hot doggies and lemonade." One of the members of the noble Staff, who had burdened me on my way down, I noticed to be the centre of attraction, and was hailed by all as Miss Welch. Then began the breath-taking races (taking only the breath of the girls who were racing), which were followed by the high leaps and jumps, in opposition to which a group of girls were strenuously making apologies for training on "Rickety Cicero," the bicycle. I then beheld armies of girls pulling against each other in a form of sport which resembled a sketch of the "Volga Boatmen."

During this performance I saw my friend, "The Silent Drama," being reeled by a certain young lady, Miss Withers by name. I think probably this will be interesting, for when appearing on the Great White Sheet, two doors down from the brilliant lights of Broadway (where swarms of Rupertslanders daily await the approach of a Broadway street car), many charming young things in berets will be seen cheering and spurring the athletes on to victory.

When my burden returned to take me (because I was tired), my running board felt that it had been a "howling" success.

T. BURT and A. GREEN.

GETTING INTO MISCHIEF

"We like to laugh; we like to have fun;
We like to chase and we like to run;
We like to climb barns"; said Sally and Ann,
"And get into mischief as much as we can."

"We like to have buggy rides out to the farm,"
Said Sally and Ann, "it does us no harm,
We tear our dresses and ruffle our hair,
But we're having fun, so we don't care."

J. REYNOLDS.
Age 10.

THE SPIRIT OF '30

(Told in 1940 to our special "Eagle" Correspondent)

Well! Here I am back in good old Alma Mater once more. It certainly feels great, but the School seems rather unnaturally silent. I wonder what's happened? I'm going upstairs now, and gracious! here's a School clock! Right at the top of the stairs. I wonder when they got that? It says ten to nine, but there is no first bell! Why? I remember when I was here somebody had an unexpressed desire for no bells, and it seems that at last it has come true. Everybody automatically goes to the room where they have First Period to deposit their books. Everybody's lining up now to go into Prayers. I think I'll go in with Form Eleven. Here we all are—Miss Millard has just come in and the air is surcharged with respect as she walks down the aisle. But what's this walking after her? A School Choir! What perfectly beautiful voices these girls have! Miss Millard isn't reading the lesson; I wonder if she has a sore throat? Oh no, here is one of the girls to read it. It certainly sounds nice to hear her. We're praying now and everyone knows the General Thanksgiving! The choir is singing an anthem which it seems to have learned under the able guidance of Miss Pauli, for its members look to her for approbation quite frequently.

We're out of Prayers now and I'm in the History room. What's become of the old Form rooms? They aren't here anyway. This is really interesting—I can positively *feel* a History atmosphere. The teacher's sitting in the middle of the room in the most convenient arm chair, which she wheels around to suit her fancy, and sits beside whoever wants help. (The girls are all sitting around her in a circle.) Each girl very chummily helps the other when it's necessary, but there is no unseemly disturbance.

I thought I'd wander into the French room and here I am. They have a piano in one corner and the girls are gathering round it to sing. They *have* got nice voices and French is such a truly musical tongue. I wish I were back here again. We never had time for things like that—we were so busy learning nasty verbs and Grammar. Of course we had our French Club, but we couldn't meet very often. It's the end of the period and such a kindly, inoffensive buzzer rings in each room.

It's recess now and I've spent an interesting time so far anyway. If only we "1930-ists" could have seen what we might have been!

After recess—I'm still wandering and I *did* find the Mathematics room interesting. The air simply reeks of figures and formulas. The Science Lab was such a nice discovery—smelly place, too.

12.30, and the buzzer in the Studio where I am now gives a friendly buzz—and I am reminded of that horrible clang in bygone days, which seemed to scream "Knock off work now," and we *did*. These people just go on working and finish their occupation and then go down to lunch. I feel the need of some sustaining nourishment greatly—all these new things have been almost too much for me.

In the noon hour some energetic souls engaged in a comparatively noiseless game of basketball. It was a marvellous game to watch.

It's 3.30 now and I spent most of the afternoon in the Kindergarten. Such a *cheerful* room, but not overpoweringly cheerful. It's all "done" in happy colours. All the other rooms had their own special colour, too. The French room was done in red—a restful and retiring red, of course, not a screaming scarlet; and so on. What has impressed me a great deal all day is the soothing silence in the corridors. Nobody seems to speak in them.

As the girls were all getting ready to go home, I accompanied them to the cloakroom and then outside. Already many of them were skimming lightly over the smooth surface of the rink and enjoying themselves, and making as much noise as possible in this voluntary exercise.

This has certainly been an instructive day, but I doubt if I shall ever survive the shock of the great change in dear old Rupert's Land.

P.

THESE I HAVE LOVED

(After Rupert Brooke)

The colourless glaze by a lamplight cast
    With vague persistence upon a dark wall;
The creakings of an old pine mast
    Bearing the weight of a sudden squall;
Sun-warmed planks to lie on after swimming;
    The lap and the lull of lazy water;
A tepid bath nearly over-brimming;
    The friendly gleam of a negro porter;
The trees and rocks surrounding a lake;
    New rubber's appetizing smell;
The sunny ripples of a swift boat's wake;
    The gurgling depths of a country well.

E. LODGE.
Age 14.

MUSIC

It is not an easy task for one who has only been teaching in the School for a space of six months to expound fully on the progress made by the girls in this particular branch of Art.

I *can* say that we are working very hard for the practical examinations of the Associated Board of the Royal Academy and Royal College of Music, London, which take place at the beginning of next term, the results of which I hope will come up to our expectations in passing with "honourable mention." The names of the candidates are as follows:

Local Centre

L. House...Rudiments Paper—"Advanced"
K. Hopps ....Rudiments Paper and Practical—"Intermediate"
A. Curry.................Rudiments Paper and Practical—"Advanced"

School

M. White ....Higher Division
M. Denison ....Lower Division
D. Donovan...Lower Division
J. Alexander...Primary Division
C. Machray...Primary Division

At the beginning of next term the girls are giving a concert, the programme of which will be comprised of part songs, duets and trios, pianoforte solos and duets. Admission will be by programme only, and the proceeds will go towards a combination Victrola-Radio, which we greatly need. This will be a great boon, especially amongst the Boarders. I hope, and I am sure it *will* create enthusiasm, interest, and a wider appreciation of music in general.

Last, but not least, we are competing for the first time in the Festival, entailing hard practice, but worth every bit of energy we are using. We have entered two classes under the heading of "School Choruses," also the "Junior Vocal Duet," "Intermediate Pianoforte Duet," and the "Intermediate Pianoforte Solo." Let's hope that the month of May is our Lucky Month!

M. HOWARD PAULI.

.Ruth Wells, who is working under Miss Gwendda Owen Davies, is taking her "Advanced" Rudiments and Practical at the Local Centre.

.Miss Georgie Lockhart is planning a recital for her Junior piano pupils. This will be given at the College near the end of May.

Miss Kershaw tells us that Evelyn Rogers and Jean MacNab are preparing for Conservatory of Music (Toronto) examinations.

SENSATIONS ON FIRST DONNING CHOIR ROBES

At last the long-looked-for day arrived, the day on which we were to sing in the choir at St. John's Cathedral for the Commemoration service. Once in the Vestry, we began to don the robes assigned to us. But alas! what a number of large people there must be in the Cathedral choir, for everything was several sizes too large. First we struggled into the cassocks; so far so good. But what of this tent-like affair called a surplice? Had it a front or hind side? From whence did one's head issue? Suddenly there was a startled yelp from one of our number, and we looked about to observe that someone had actually managed to get all the parts of her costume on. It was M———, who is small and round-faced. She was completely swallowed up in the voluminous folds of her robes, and her small, anxious face peered forth from behind the tassel of a large teetering mortar-board. It was too much. The whole choir collapsed on the floor or benches in a complete and blissful state of hysterics.

THE HOUSE SYSTEM

The girls have certainly shown a great deal of interest in the introduction of the "House" system which, for the benefit of the uninitiated, may be described as a "group" system. From Form IV upwards the girls are divided into four equal groups, each of which contains approximately the same number of girls from each Form. These groups bear the names of persons intimately connected with the School. We have Matheson House, in honour of His Grace the Archbishop of Rupert's Land. Machray House reminds us of that other Archbishop whose name is so well known in Winnipeg. Miss Dalton, a former Head Mistress of the School, has kindly given permission for her name to be used for another of the Houses; while the fourth bears the name Eva L. Jones. It is quite likely, and peculiarly appropriate, that the last-named House will win, for the year 1929-30, the shield very kindly presented by Mrs. Glennie for inter-house competition.

All sides of School life feature in the contest; points are awarded for School work, conduct, deportment, gymnastics, field day activities, and games. The Houses vie with each other in the production of concerts, which have already revealed unexpected talent. As the various activities have been described elsewhere by the House Secretaries, it is only necessary to conclude that the system has proved a great success and that the healthy spirit of competition which has been introduced is encouraging each girl to make a special effort to improve the standard of her work.

HOUSE NOTES

EVA L. JONES HOUSE

Captains	MISS HOLDITCH, MISS LORING
Lieutenants	MISS WELCH, MISS PAULI, JOCELYN BOTTERELL
Secretary	BEATRICE MCMEANS
Entertainment Organizer	ELEANOR LODGE
Drill Captain	MARY WHITLEY
Games Captain	AUDREY GARLAND

Eva L. Jones was the name given us at the solemn Christening Ceremony, when our youngest member, Lois O'Grady, was carried in by her godparents and dumped in a bath to represent the House being christened, while the rest of the House, standing in horse-shoe formation, joined in the ceremony ably conducted by Priest Starkey. After the christening all the members of the House enjoyed tea, provided by the

EVA L. JONES DRILL EIGHT

House Captains and Lieutenants. With dancing and music we spent a jolly afternoon.

We are thrilled with our name, and aim to live up to the thoughts it suggests—an all-round development of every talent each of us possesses, with the heights as our goal, as suggested by our School Motto, "Alta Petens." By combined hard work and good fortune our House has come first at every opportunity, and the shield in the hall is warned to prepare itself for the honour of bearing our name on its silver surface —providing our good luck continues.

Sports Day did not prove to be a feather in our cap; however, next day, in the Drill Competition, we successfully redeemed our reputation. We congratulate our Senior Drill Eight, for this made us the successful House when the first month's totals were announced. The proud members of Eva

L. Jones were determined to keep this position, but in the following months the other Houses have shown us what close rivals we have in School marks, and it is due to the care and determination of our Boarders not to lose the order and neatness marks allotted to each House—and to keep their belongings in their care instead of letting "Pound" borrow them—that we have been able to retain our much-coveted position.

At the Annual Tea and Gift Shop in aid of the Zenana Mission, our House, with Machray House, was allotted the Gift Shop, at which we had the leather, brass, fancy goods and needlework stalls, and the fishpond, all of which contributed well to the amount raised.

Our Games and Drill Captains have been very energetic in coaching our House basketball teams. Dalton and Eva L. Jones were the first to meet in a House contest. We were the successful ones this time. Let's hope that our good luck will stay with us in the cup matches to be played at the end of the season.

"Let's be original" is not the motto of our House, but it was on the day of our entertainment—the original work of our capable stage manager, Eleanor Lodge. Our thanks are due to Miss Welch and our versatile accompanist, Miss Pauli, who freely gave of their time to help us make it a success. The Juniors, after introducing themselves in a lively chorus, served tea to the guests. A clever skit on School topics, composed by Miss Welch, was sung by a chorus of Seniors, who also "twisted their toes" in between the verses. Two Parsons arrived to visit the girls, and sang, amid peals of laughter—for these Parsons proved to be Miss Pauli and Miss Welch!! Our youngest members did their part with games, songs and dances. Evelyn Rogers in her acrobatic dance, and Margaret McNabb in a charming lullaby, and also playing tunes on milk bottles, were much applauded. Our entertainment concluded with an original play, "School Girls We," written and produced by Eleanor Lodge. The cast did adequate justice to this well-thought-out skit on school life which combined Gilbert and Sullivan humour with their well-known tunes. All the girls were unanimous in their good opinion of our performance, and Jean Wells as "Head Mistress" will not soon be forgotten. Thanks to the support of the other Houses, we were able to send, as a result of our efforts, $25 to the Eva L. Jones Memorial Fund.

We must not omit our appreciation of the delightful Tea given by our Captain, Miss Holditch, for the many members of the House.

Good luck to all our members—those who are leaving us, and those who will be here to carry on the good work next year.

DALTON HOUSE

Captain..MISS BANNISTER
Lieutenants...............................MISS SHELDON, MISS JOHNSON,
TERRY BURT
Secretary ....MARION SMITH

Dalton House received from Miss Dalton, a former Principal of the School, and from whom we got our name, a scholarship of $25 for the neatest girl in the House. She also very kindly sent a photograph, which is to be put up next to the House notices.

We started the School year merrily by tying first place with two other Houses at the House Meet held at Sargent Park. At the first meeting the Sports Captain, Secretary, and Entertainment Committee were elected. A motto was suggested by Miss Dalton, which everybody agreed upon: "The merit of one

DALTON HOUSE RELAY TEAM

is the honour of all." There were the drill contests, in which the Seniors came second and first and the Juniors third. This added considerably to the House points.

Immediately after Christmas, preparations were made for the concert, which was held on April 4th. One of the most appreciated items on the programme was the movie of the Sports Meet, which was kindly loaned and operated by Dorothy Wither. Among other items on the programme were a "Mock Trial" in rhyme written by Miss Bannister, and a Toy Parliament by the Juniors. The concert was brought to an end by the Dalton House song, written by Miss Johnson to the tune of "Forty Years On." Having ended a very successful year, we look forward to greater success in the future.

MATHESON HOUSE

Captain	MISS SCHŒNAU
Lieutenants	MISS SHORT, MISS MOSS,
	R. WELLS
Secretary	M. BARTLETT
Games Captain	N. WHITLEY
Entertainment Organizer	D. BAINS

Matheson House, which takes its name from that old and honoured friend of the College, His Grace, the Archbishop of Rupert's Land, has for its Captain Miss Schœnau. Its Lieutenants are Miss Moss, Miss Short and Ruth Wells. At the meetings this year, both at those with and without the Staff members present, our aim has been to promote House spirit and increase co-operation between the Juniors and Seniors in the House. So far the House has not distinguished itself in the competition for the shield, but we go on working in the hope that "the last may be first."

On September 27th we held a Birthday Party at River Park. Combining work with pleasure, we ran races and chose those who were to represent us on Sports Day. We then proceeded to a more secluded spot. Although there were a few splatters of rain at first, these stopped by the time we had collected firewood, and we soon forgot the grey skies while toasting wieners and bacon, as well as our faces, over a large bonfire.

Matheson House took charge of the tea when the Annual Tea and Sale of Work in aid of the Zenana Guild was held on November 16th. About one-half of the hall was shut off by a line of benches, and here the girls, wearing yellow aprons and tiny round hats of back and yellow, served tea to the guests.

Our House Entertainment took the form of a St. Patrick's Tea Party on March 17th. After tea had been served, the guests amused each other, as they were all ordered to do different things. First came a Junior peanut race and then the Senior, and last, a race between the winners, Eleanor Lodge and Clementina Adamson. Miss Welch then put the Staff through a table of Swedish exercises, which occasioned much merriment. Two groups of girls acted charades, and then twelve or thirteen Seniors, dressed in pyjama trousers, blazers many sizes too small for them, and tall black hats, gave their version of "Ten Little Nigger Boys," the dance originally performed by the Babies' dancing class. This brought the Tea to a hilarious conclusion.

MACHRAY HOUSE

Captain...MISS PEARMAN
Lieutenants...MISS JONES, MISS CHUBB,
P. MURPHY
Secretary..P. MURPHY
Games Captain ....A. GREEN

At the first meeting of our House Miss Pearman explained the House system for the benefit of the Juniors. The Lieutenants took this opportunity of becoming acquainted with the members of the House. Suggestions for a House motto were given, but as these were not numerous and the choice was not unanimous, it was decided to leave this important matter until some later date when Machray House might perhaps have developed a character of its own.

We were the first people to give a House entertainment, which took the form of a concert ending up with a one-act play. All parts of the House were represented in the various dances and recitations, which caused a great deal of amusement. Seniors took part in "The Rest Cure," a play in which Dorothy Champion played the part of the neurotic author taking a rest cure. Vera Fryer was his long-suffering wife, while Mary Lile Love and Jane Nicholls were the somewhat hard-hearted nurses. Ruth Fletcher was the essentially practical "maid of all work," who aided and abetted the author in his escape from the nursing home when he made up his mind that he no longer needed a rest cure.

The Field Day was the first competitive event in which the Houses took part and it aroused a great deal of enthusiasm. Machray girls secured first place with Matheson and Dalton Houses. We have done well in the drill competitions and Audrey Green is largely responsible for this success, as she has taken considerable trouble over the training of the drill eights.

In School work we began by being bottom but by Easter reached first place, although we have not yet succeeded in beating Eva L. Jones House on totals for the year. If our Juniors endeavour to reduce the number of order marks still more after the Summer holiday PERHAPS we shall have better luck next year.

As we approach the close of the first year under the House system at Rupert's Land we find ourselves wiser in many ways after keen competition with the other Houses and we are looking forward to developing a still stronger enthusiasm for House and School in future days.

Snap Shots and Autographs

Betty?

Campbell

Leilah Florance

Snap Shots and Autographs

mara

W   o our Friend

Fork

Mary

Pat P

J

TOKYO

I have never seen Tokyo, but I can imagine Tokyo in Spring.

Peachy-coloured azaleas are blooming under the balconies in rocky beds, and small snails are crawling among the mossy rocks as I walk slowly on to Yan-Pun's humble abode, through the narrow, winding street, listening to the sweet song of the nightingale. The air is sweet with the gentle perfume of the cherry blossoms overhead. From the mountains the winds softly blow. "I tramp along in silence, for what song of mine could make such a music as the Spring winds' song." A little frog is hopping along with me, the butterflies are fluttering in the clear blue sky.

The nightingale is singing in the plum flowers, but alas, his song is disturbed as the "bean cake peddler comes bawling along," crying his wares in a piercing tongue, and pleading with his soft gray eyes. I buy a cake and munch it while I listen again to the nightingale.

"Far across hill and dale the plum blossoms have cast a delicate veil." "I look up, and lo, the plum tree petals scatter down a fall of purest snow."

Now I am passing a group of children squabbling over kites, and selling tiny crickets in real cages. The crickets are singing and chirping. Such a commotion!

A sudden shower, people thinking in a hurry how to cover up their heads. Two friends are walking in raincoats and chattering gaily under an umbrella. I must hop into a rickshaw. But now the rain has stopped, I will stay in the rickshaw because the streets are wet.

I am passing a rich man's house. Two little boys are out sweeping the blossoms up, but some children are calling and telling them to spare the blossoms. A little maiden is complaining because she has just cleaned and swept, and down more camellias fall.

Now I am going over a bridge; the midges are humming all around. Willows are hanging over the stream and the fish rise out of the stream to snap at dragon-flies. Far away I see people setting out rice-plants. The king-fisher is pluming his wings in the stream and ducks are sailing along. A beautiful pheasant, "his tail dragging like a mountain trail," is majestically walking on the bank. Pear blossoms hang over the bridge. Men are fishing in the stream and shouting delightedly over their catches.

But here I am at the house of my friend. A house of the middle-class man. Wisterias climb over the fence and poppies bloom at the gate. I walk through the gate in wonder. The garden, such a garden! Flowers everywhere, crocuses, daffodils, lilies, irises and lotuses. A little fly, wet with the rain, heavy drooping wings, crawls slowly up the gate post. Rabbits are playing with chestnuts under the trees. A weasel slips in and out of the clover.

My host is at the door ready to greet me. He ushers me into a room, sweet with incense, and bids me sit on the floor. A small boy clatters in with a tray, on which two teapots stand. He puts one in front of each of us. Another boy brings in bowls of rice and chopsticks. We eat; drink out of the teapot spout, and chat gaily in Japanese. Yan tells me that this is the night of the Lantern Festival and that men are now adorning his house with paper lanterns.. I will not take time to tell about the Lantern Festival's origin, but I will say that it is a time when everyone decorates his house and carries lanterns of every shape all round the city at dark.

At last I must leave. It is now dusk and fireflies are beginning to light their lamps. As I cross the bridge the fireflies in the water plants look like water flowers.

The moon is out now and the moths are dancing on the moors. Bats are flitting down beneath the bridge. The frogs are beginning to call and the stars are out. "The mirrored image of the moon is a pillow for the birds that float asleep upon the stream." The night wind sings through the willows. The night is quiet and cool. As yet people have not come out with their lanterns. The crane is asleep, though still standing on one foot. The foxes slink through the rice fields. Again, the air is sweet with perfume of all the flowers.

Now, one by one the people are coming with their lanterns. I never saw anything so beautiful before; dim silhouettes slowly moving along, high above them floating lighted flowers, birds, fish and every manner of thing. Boats are drifting in the stream with lanterns in their sterns and prows.

I am on the crooked street again. I, too, purchase some lanterns to carry. The temple bells are filling the air with music. Above the music I hear shouts and laughter; barks of tiny Japanese dogs as they bite at the worrying lanterns around their necks; the liquid notes of the nightingale over my head. Even the glow-worms join in the merry-making with their lanterns.

I feel that I must stay out all night to watch the Festival. "All night long the dance goes on, till dew upon the dancers' sleeves proclaims that it is dawn."

> "In the ocean of the sky
> Borne on waves of cloud,
> The moon ship
> Goes a-gliding by
> Through a forest of stars."

At last the sun rises. People are now disappearing into their doors. The dew is like stars that have fallen in the night. "An early morning breeze; yes, and a single goose up in the rose clouds, nothing more." The spider webs are glistening in the dawn. The chrysanthemums are like

"Prisoned moonbeams
Caught in an early frost."

and I thought I saw a crimson petal arise from a poppy, but 'twas only a butterfly.

Then the children start off to school and the excitement is over for another year.

M. LAIRD.

THE SAILOR'S SONG

The Captain of a ship am I,
In which I sail under the deep blue sky.
A hundred men are at my command
Who take my ship from land to land.
I've been right round the great wide world,
Over seas that are calm and curled.

Many are the sights my eyes have seen,
Many the suns under which I've been.
I've seen a thousand different seas
And a million kinds of trees.
I've been right round the great wide world,
Over seas that are calm and curled.

RUTH HOSKIN.
Age 12.

TO A HORSE

Bess, you have a shining coat
And a frisky black colt,
That follows you where ever you go,
To or fro.

You trot gently and easily,
And gallop steadily and leisurely;
While behind comes your colt,
Like a goat.

While you graze in the pasture
And show your beautiful figure,
The sun shines on your coat
Showing as gold.

When you in your harness I see,
I think to myself what I saw,
Your head so high and stately,
And you so shapely.

P. ROBINSON.

SEA-GULL

The soul of a sailor buried at sea
Is high in the blue sky looking at me
While I lean on the rail of my ship.

As I watch its flight, and its sloping wings,
And its home on the rocks where the wet spray clings,
I am glad for that soul on the sea.

It forgets tramp-steamers, and tavern lights,
And grey, dirty decks and vague harbour-lights,
And the terror of slippery masts.

But it lives with wide breeze-blown clouds and waves,
Loving quiet beaches, and dim misty caves,
And the freedom of galloping seas.

SHEILA CAMPBELL.
Age 16.

SOMETHING'S WRONG!

A humming, droning, buzzing, persistent uproar floated along the corridor, and invaded the peaceful quiet of the front hall. Learned ears heard, learned brows frowned, learned lips formed the words "something's wrong!" and learned feet walked unerringly towards Form IX. Questioning eyes and innocent faces turn towards the open door. Was it that their maidenly chatter was troublesome, or their playful laughter annoying at all? Oh! the bell has gone! Black legs cease from "seeking the heights," desk-seats clang, and hot hands clasp wrinkled foreheads, as studies commence. Form IX is perfectly silent. "Something's wrong," thinks Miss Schœnau as she opens her Maths.

We should congratulate Miss Schœnau on passing through the past tempestuous year without being completely prostrated. She must welcome the thought of the holiday as a ship-wrecked sailor on a stormy sea would welcome the sight of a sunny island.

The Prefects elected this year were Eva Mary Adamson and Sheila Campbell. Grey hairs are not to be mentioned in their hearing. Sometimes, when they take a study period, Eva Mary's face reddens with suppressed excitement—"they are actually working!" An ominous silence reigns round Jane's desk—"Something's wrong," thinks Sheila.

Sports and other activities play an important part in Form IX. A treasured possession is Nora Whitley, who plays on the First Basketball Team, and the Second Team is represented by Betty Snell and Ruth Inkster. Dancing is eagerly attended every week by several "Form fairies," and there is a bustle when "gym" is announced.

The House system has rather divided the Form up, of course, but it has also done much to introduce a very patriotic spirit and invitations for teas and entertainments have proved very popular (we respond joyfully to every one), and members from E. L. Jones, Machray, Matheson and Dalton strive in friendly battle to win top honours for their House.

Yet our carefree chatter and girlish laughter will not disturb the peace much longer, and all those with tingling nerves and shattered ear-drums may relax with a sigh of relief —for our days are darkened by the thoughts of June exams, and soon we shall sink into a blissful state of coma, with printed paper and reams of foolscap pushed before our uncomprehending eyes. Some will never really awake from this dream—but we all hope to recover slowly from the shock, and even now some brave souls are studying hard at odd moments, and sudden remembrance sobers our hilarity, so that we stagger to our desk and gaze with resolute eyes on the cold print at a Latin or History book—while silence reigns. Miss Schœnau peers round the door, and smothers a startled exclamation. "Something's wrong," she murmurs, as she flees down the corridor.

DAWN

Dawn in her golden chariot
  Rides swiftly over the land,
Which at her bidding soon will wake
  By the touch of her magic hand.
She is clothed in a robe of silver,
  At her back flows a wonderful train,
And if this train should turn to grey,
  It's the sign of a shower of rain.
Her chariot is drawn headlong,
  By a pair of golden steeds,
With wings of shining silver and gold,
  And hair like golden reeds.

J. MALCOLMSON.
Age 13.

FRENCH CLUB

A French Club has been formed at the request of many girls in Form X who are anxious for conversation. Miss Millard was elected Honorary President and Miss Sheldon, President.

The meetings are held once a month to hear a lecture in French, and the one given by Monsieur de la Lande on "Les Parfums" was much appreciated.

Refreshments are served after each meeting and many thanks are offered to Miss Millard and those parents who so kindly sent us the cakes.

Examinations and other School activities have been the cause of several postponed meetings this term, but we intend to carry on with even greater enthusiasm and success next September.

P. WEBB,
Secretary.

AQUAS CALIENTES

"Aquas Calientes"—hear its tempting sound,
"Hot waters"—how it makes me yearn
    To view its beauty.
Romantic maids with careless graces,
Showing the witchery of their fair race,
Stately grace displayed in their mantillas,
    Turn wheresoe'er I may,
    By night or day,
I see the lazy beauty and romance of the South.

The balconies peep curiously, and almost fall
Into the street they long to see,
    They've iron bonds.
Lovers pluck tranquilly the strings
Of their guitars, and shyly sing their love.
Maidens peep fearfully from behind the bars
    That prison all the windows,
    Poor, yearning lovers,
Their love is light, on the morrow they'll another woo.

The curious, subdued murmur of distant voices,
The lazy hum of drowsy insects
    Pervades the air.
The listless péon strolls along
The ill-paved lanes, where house-tops almost touch,
And barter scandal with malicious glee.
    Sky eternally blue,
    Unmarred by clouds,
The water reflects brilliantly the dazzling blue of heaven.

I long for the day when I shall see thee,
Beautiful, tempting, unseen Aquas Calientes.

M. L. LOVE.
Age 15

At the end of last year we were very sorry to lose our Sports Captain, Nancy Milton. She had been at the College many years and had proved herself to be a valuable person in sports. It seems late in the year now to congratulate Mary Whitley, who was elected to take Nancy's place, but this is the first chance that we have had to do so. Nancy's shoes were big ones to fill!! but Mary was evidently the right person. She has been a great help and a very reliable Captain. Congratulations are also due to Norah Whitley and Norrie Jacob for obtaining their "B's" for the First School Team and to Betty Snell, Jean Wells, Ruth Inkster and Bernice Patterson for winning places on the Second Team.

Basketball

The basketball of the School has kept at the same high standard that it reached last year, and the House system being introduced into the School, a keen, competitive spirit was

First Basketball Team and Coach

created, as the games are now played in Houses and no longer in Forms. Each House elected its own Games Captain, and these Captains have been responsible for coaching the younger members of the Houses. I should like to thank these four girls—Audrey Garland, Audrey Green, Norah Whitley and Kathleen Hopps—for all the assistance that they have given me.

The Eva L. Jones House was the first one to send in a challenge—they chose Dalton House for their opponents. It was a good game and resulted in a win for Jones House.

The first "outside" match of the season caused great excitement—it was against Riverbend School. Our opponents accepted our challenge and came to the College to play. The game was played before a great number of spectators. It was a hard game and Riverbend put up a splendid fight. The game ended with the score 51-9 in favour of the College. After the game we entertained our guests at tea.

On March 20th the First and Second School Teams played against each other. It was an excellent game. The First Team scored heavily over the Second, but at the same time the Second Team played up well and were by no means trodden

SECOND BASKETBALL TEAM

on. After the match we all had tea together in the Assembly Hall. After the "basketball" appetites had been satisfied, the girls evidently thought that a fortune teller was entertaining them, for numerous teacups were passed up to the end of the table! Whether or not the truth was told remains to be seen; fortunately I knew some of the dark secrets of their lives! so there are still hopes that my reputation as a "teacup reader" will not be entirely lost!

We received a challenge from Riverbend School for a return match, and we played this at Westminster Hall. Unfortunately, owing to lack of space, we were able to take only a limited number of spectators. Our opponents showed much improvement in their play and they gave us a good game. The match resulted in a win for the College again, the score being 45-22. After the match, Miss Foster, members of the Staff, and the Riverbend Team entertained us at tea. It was a very enjoyable afternoon.

On March 28th both our First and Second Teams played against teams from the Norwood Collegiate. K. Hopps substituted for B. Patterson and played splendidly. Our teams played an excellent game. Great credit is due to Audrey Garland, who shot fourteen out of the seventeen baskets that the College scored. The results were: First Team 34-17, Second Team 28-22.

On the following Saturday we played against the Old Girls. This was one of the most enjoyable matches of the season. We were rather nervous, as they had several girls on their team who played on the School Team last year. Both First and Second Teams played an excellent game, but the Second Team especially played a most spectacular game in passing. All our forwards were in great form. After the match we all enjoyed coffee and cakes. It is very gratifying to end. a season not having lost a match, and to have such a splendid Second Team.

Skating

This year only a small rink was made; it was chiefly meant for the younger members of our family, and for the Boarders. The rink was not completed until late in the season, so it did not give us long to skate.

Swimming

No, it was not compulsory! but one might have thought so from the numbers that arrived every week to swim at the Cornish Baths. It was quite a new adventure for the College, but it proved to be a successful one.

At the end of the season some of the girls took their Royal Life Saving Examinations. All the candidates were successful.

Elementary Certificate. — Eva Mary Adamson, Julia Adamson.

Proficiency Certificate.—Nancy Milton, Margaret Shepley, Betty Snell, Elizabeth Wright, Betty Ross, Ruth Glassco, Elaine Henderson, Eleanor Lodge, Mary Lile Love.

Bronze Medallion.—Eleanor Lodge, Ruth Glassco, Elaine Henderson, Mary Stephens.

Tennis

Last year we became the proud possessors of a new hard court. It was made during the Summer vacation, so we have not had much time to play on it. However, we have tested it and are now waiting for the snow to disappear so that we can start to train as tennis stars!

LILIAN M. WELCH.

TEAM CRITICISMS

A great spirit has been shown throughout the year in both the First and Second School Teams. I hope this public spirit is so deeply rooted in the College now that we shall never lose it, and that the Juniors of the School will keep up the standard that the Seniors have set them.

The First and Second Teams this year are composed of girls whom we are very proud to have with us in the School, and each one has contributed her best throughout the season, making it a very successful one.

First Team

Right Forward, NORAH WHITLEY.—A steady and reliable player.

Left Forward, AUDREY GARLAND.—A great asset to her team; is a strong player and has done excellent work.

Running Centre, AUDREY GREEN.—Has a great team spirit and can always be relied upon.

Jumping Centre, PHYLLIS WEBB.—Generally plays an excellent game; at times unsteady.

Guard, MARGARET BARTLETT.—Strong and steady; plays a good game.

Guard, NORRIE JACOB.—Tremendous improvement shown during season; works hard.

Second Team

Right Forward, BERNICE PATTERSON.—An excellent worker; erratic, and shots need care.

Left Forward, BETTY SNELL.—Very keen; a quick player, but not steady at present.

Jumping Centre, JEAN WELLS.—Must learn to keep cool. Too excitable to be steady; with more experience should do well.

Running Centre, MARY WHITLEY.—An excellent Captain and a reliable player.

Guard, VIOLA GLENNIE.—Sticks well and plays an energetic game.

Guard, RUTH INKSTER.—Worked well and forms a strong defence with other guard.

FORM X DEBATE

On March 19th there was a debate in Form X to discuss whether poverty is a spur or a bar to achievement. Miss Jones acted as Chairman, and the motion was resolved by Jean Wells and seconded by Kathleen Moore. The motion was opposed by Phyllis Webb and Mary Lile Love.

At first it looked as though the opposers of the motion would be in the majority, but when some very persuasive points were brought out by the proposers, one could almost see minds being changed. Jean's argument was that achievement demands exertion, toil and sacrifice. Examples of this are Beethoven and Handel, who were poor in the first place; who became musicians whose work is known the world over; yet who achieved their great purpose in life despite poverty. Oliver Goldsmith is another example: he had to sell his "Deserted Village" in order to pay his rent.

Another point was that the struggle in early life for the bare necessities gives an individual the true sense of value, carefulness and resources necessary for success, also proving that poverty is the mother of invention.

The last thrust was that poverty means plain food and clothing, and plain living, which leads to a sound mind in a sound body.

Our opponents had many points against us, the first of which was that great masters of music and literature could have done a great deal more if they had not been harrassed over financial matters; but we think that poverty was their spur.

Their argument against our second point was that poor people who have worked for money all their life do not know how to use it; but it is only an exceptional person, who has had to be careful of money all his life, who uses it unwisely.

The point about plain living was objected to strongly. It was pointed out to us that poor people become degraded, warped, and evil because of their wretched surroundings, poor food and medical attention. Our argument was that the poor are used to the hardships of life and can withstand them better than those who grow up in luxury and ease. We gave an example of a woodcutter who goes to the outside of a forest for a strong tree which has been exposed to adverse conditions, and not to the ones in the centre which have been sheltered all their lives.

After these points had been duly criticised and discussed by both sides, a vote was taken, and the resolution that Poverty is a Spur and Not a Bar to Achievement won a majority of seven votes—20-13.

JEAN WELLS.

I LOOKED THROUGH THE BRAMBLES

On a couch of moss with a cover of briar roses lay the most lovely lady; her hair was like sunbeams on a river, her eyes were as blue as a Summer sky. She was as fresh as a primrose and as sweet as a sweet pea. Her lips were as red as a rose and her hands as delicate as harebells. Her cheeks were as pink as a wild rose, her dress looked as if it were made of violet petals embroidered with roses in gold.

At her feet lay a pretty little deer, and a beautiful bluebird sang above her. A stream bubbled past and little daisies dotted the grass. A little breeze kissed her cheek and whispered in her ear, "Wake up, wake up."

The stream bubbled, "Look, look—look who has come."

Slowly she woke up and saw me; but just then who should come but a handsome prince; his curly fair hair tumbled over his shoulders. He lifted her up and vanished with her.

I was in bed and it was only a dream.

P. JARMAN.
Age 8.

THE MAGIC CARPET

All Olympus was in an upheaval. A mortal was to be chosen to become one of the gods. Odin said the one to be chosen must follow some occupation that made the earth a more interesting, a more magical place in which to live.

One by one each god took his turn trying to find the right mortal. Frey chose a builder of ships, for, said he, "Nothing is more exciting than a sea voyage." The choice of Poseidon, the god of the sea, fell on the inventor of a diving suit. "What," he exclaimed, "can compare with the mystery and glory of the sea floor?" Diana, the goddess of the chase, wished the honour to be given to a hunter, for, to her, his adventures offered the greatest allure. Idun, the keeper of the life-giving apples, selected a doctor. "Why," she cried, "what magic lies in the skill and healing herbs of the doctor." A heavy rumble as of thunder was heard, and the whole earth shook with vibrations of Thor's voice, as he said, "A great general so easily is the most interesting person on earth; surely he does the most exciting things." Then Venus whispered low and sweet, "The innocent heart of a little child is earth's greatest miracle." Softly as a zephyr wind was borne the voice of the poet, Bragi: "Give me above all the weaver—whether it is the weaver of dreams, or the weaver of magic carpets. Those carpets into which are interwoven the aspirations, the dreams, and the life story of the weaver."

49

Odin pondered deeply for some moments.   Then he said,
"Bragi has chosen well.   The ships are very often drawn to destruction.   The diver alone rejoices in the beauties of the sea-
floor, but he cannot show its beauties to whom he will.   The
hunter brings fear and destruction in his wake, while the doctor
cannot always ward off death.   The general often meets defeat.
The child's heart does not always remain innocent.   But the
magic weaver—to him is given the prize.   For it is he who
weaves into his carpets the story of a life, the story of a
people, the stories of all nations.   Those stories which are
for now and for all time."

BETTY MORRISON.

FOOTSTEPS

Donald squirmed uneasily in his lair under the bed.   Why
didn't Dad hurry home and find the garage window he had
broken with his sling-shot?   It wasn't his fault, but Dad
would take his sling-shot and send him to bed without any
tea.   He'd go down and get some cookies from Janet, the new,
kind kitchen maid, and then he wouldn't be so hungry.

But now he couldn't go.   Someone was coming up the
stairs.   Someone with a slow, lumbering tread that made the
very stairs creak in pain.   That was Mathilda, the stupendous
German cook, who rolled in fat and whose body was like some
dirty, greasy dough rolled into a shape, with great rings of fat
hanging from her chin.   Donald didn't like Mathilda, because
she reminded him of stew, and he didn't like stew.

Now Janet was coming upstairs.   Janet with her hurried,
timid tread that reminded you of some frightened animal.
Janet had a tiny, willowy body, with skinny legs that made her
feet look as if they belonged to someone else.   There was
always something moving on Janet—her hands or her fluffy
golden hair that stood out in defiant curls that would not stay
straight and always seemed to quiver.   He would ask her now
for some cookies.   But Mathilda was coming down again, so
he had better not.   He settled down in a remorseful heap and
he wished he had never seen a sling-shot or a garage window.

Now he could hear the door bang and Aunt Myra's harsh
voice talking to Uncle Willie Fred—Aunt Myra insisted that
he was Uncle William Frederick, as Willie Fred did not befit
his dignity and position—and Jonathan.   Aunt Myra called
once or twice and then came marching upstairs.   There was no
hesitation in her tread.   Grim determination was portrayed
in each step.   She always walked like that and she would do
so in a fire or going to her death, with nary a falter.   She
even exceeded the expectations gained from her tread.   She
was a tall, angular woman, with sharp eyes; a straight, mas-

50

culine nose; a straight line for her grim, stern, tightly-compressed lips; a square, determined jaw, and invariably a poke bonnet. She was every child's idea of an old-fashioned schoolmarm.

Nobody could imagine why Uncle Willie Fred married Aunt Myra. He was so quiet and utterly the opposite to her. His tread was a shadow of Aunt Myra's. A little timid tread like Janet's, but not nervous, only quiet and retiring like himself.

Then came Jonathan, Aunt Myra's beloved boy. His tread was a slip-shod, shambly tread that could never hurry because it didn't know how; a watery tread with no character in it. Jonathan was a tall, angular boy like his mother. He had a plump face; hair the color of dirty wood which has been left out in the rain; watery blue eyes that never had any expression in them; a weak, full mouth that was usually open, and a very undecided chin. His hands and legs were longer than his body and hung and swung around like branches broken from a tree but not completely severed. Jonathan was a sissy in Donald's eyes; a sleepy, lazy, dumb sissy that nobody need bother about, and Donald didn't bother.

Now Mummy had come in, Dad was putting the car away and would be sure to see the hole, and, hearing Aunt Myra's forceful voice, was coming up to see her. Donald loved Mummy's tread. It was such a soft, gentle, loving and yet dignified tread, with quite as much character in it as Aunt Myra's, but yet suggesting dainty, graceful, sweet-faced Mummy with her lovely golden-brown hair falling in caressing waves around her face.

But now Dad was coming upstairs in a hard, angry stamp and Donald knew that it was the end.

EILEEN CHANDLER.
Age 14.

Elaine (eating a box of loose-leaf reinforcements)—"These life-savers don't taste like they used to."

JONAH AND THE WHALE

RUTH WELLS.
Age 18.

This year we have had many enthusiastic and keen workers in the studio, who have all done their share in adding colour and brightness to the studio walls.

Our problem and abstract pictures have caused many remarks of wonder and admiration.

Everyone has shown an interest in the House, which is rapidly assuming a "desirable furnished residence" look, owing to united efforts.

We shall all be sorry when Ruth is no longer here to shed her usual atmosphere of silent enthusiasm.

Owing to the scarcity of Art exhibitions in the city this year, the Studio Club has only been to see two. The first, held at the Hudson's Bay store on September 30th, was one sponsored by the British Institute of Industrial Art, and the exhibits which were sent over from England, were most varied and interesting. Some of us were fascinated by pottery and woodwork, and others amused themselves by looking at linecuts and leather-work, while still others were discovering book illustrations and carved toys. We enjoyed the display so much that the Art classes throughout the School were taken to see it at intervals during the week it was on view.

The last exhibition that we saw was of water colours by members of the Winnipeg Sketching Club. Although most of the pictures were scenes from the Lake of the Woods district and Manitoba, there were several scenes of the mountains and Western Canada that aroused much admiration.

THE STUDIO TEA

We like High tea in the Studio,
    High stools for us, too.
    Shrimp salad steeped in dressing,
    And ice-cream "poured," we do.

We like Tea poured for the first hour
    Even by Miss Short.
    Miss Millard spoke of a new scheme
    For Summer, sea-sport.

We like Dodgy's new poems,
    And actions that we saw.
    Her stable-yard contortions
    Caused many to hee-haw.

We like Artistic criticisms,
    But only if they're sweet,
    Then we wash those sticky dishes,
    And leave our studio neat.

                   E. LODGE.

GREAT EXPECTATIONS

The girls of our little community are very sunny under the supervision of Miss Bannister; they form the nucleus of what, it is hoped, will prove to be very bright specimens of humanity. Everyone keeps smiling, although it must be confessed that a few individuals occasionally "smile" rather too vigorously at the wrong moment.

On the last day of the Christmas Term we had a toboggan party. About four members of the Staff were there and after an hour's fun we went to the "Corner Cupboard" for a meal which proved rather disappointing. Form matches have been replaced by House matches, so we have no sports news to give.

The most outstanding feat accomplished by this equally outstanding Form was when it led the School in singing Hymn 112 under the direction of Miss Pauli. The class is quite optimistic with regard to the formation of a School choir next year and it is hoped that it will consist chiefly of these future Form XI girls. As we are nearing the end of the School year we desire to give our thanks and best wishes to Miss Millard and the Staff.

The annual Form X Dinner in honour of the graduating class is to take place on May 31st. Members of the Ladies' Board and the parents of Form XI girls are to be invited to come after dinner and spend the evening at the School.

                  PHYLLIS WEBB,
             Form X Magazine Representative.

SAILING

Sailing is a favourite sport. Every Saturday at Kenora, over at the Yacht Club, the boats are in the water ready to start. They are the thirty-two footers.

All the people are waiting to watch the race. The man in the watch-house has just fired the gun. The boats are off. The people cheer for their own boat, so people all are saying different things. There is a good breeze and the boats are going along at a good pace.

Sometimes the boats are right over on the side and will almost upset.

One boat is around the first buoy, but you cannot see who it is, as they are far away. One or two boats have got in the calm of the lake and they are very still, but suddenly they start forward as the breeze ruffles the lake. Most of the boats are rounding the second buoy and are keeping pretty well together. The people cheer and the crews in the boats call back, but the wind is dying down and the boats are going slower and slower.

The crews put up the jib and the wind is filling the sails and the boats start again. The Westing's boat is second but is quickly catching up. Now it is even with the other and they are running smoothly along. They are very close to the finish but the Westing's boat makes a sudden spurt and crosses the line.

The people congratulate the sailors and then they leave for home in their different boats, having had a nice time at the races.

Christine Machray.
Age 11.

THE NEEDLE AND THREAD

"Hurry up Mr. Thread," said the sharp little needle.

"But I can't. Can't you see I'm too fat to get through your mean little hole? Why isn't your eye bigger? What are we going to do anyway?"

"See that pink cloth over there? We are going to make that into a little dress. Hurry up now."

"Hurry, hurry, I'm always hurrying. I might get through your old hole if you'd stop dancing around. There now, that's better. I'm through at last. Ouch, that old lady's hurting me! She put a knot in my tail."

"Come along," said the bright little needle, "we are ready now. If you wouldn't snarl so we'd get there faster."

"I can't help snarling; you make me when you twist me so. This is like follow the leader: you go first and I come after. I wish I could go first sometimes. I can do more than you anyway. See that fine seam I'm holding together."

"If it weren't for me you wouldn't be where you are now," said the needle, "so good-bye. I hope the next thread won't be so grumpy.'

"Same to you," shouted out the thread.

MARY GREIG.

Form VII.

"NEWS" IN THE KINDERGARTEN

The few minutes which intervene between our short prayers and the departure of Form I to their superior (as they think) room, are taken up by "news." Monday morning is generally the most exciting, as almost everyone has been doing something thrilling during the week-end, perhaps skating or seeing a show. I attempted one morning to record the various items of the day's bulletin, with the following result:

CALVIN: I went to a show yesterday and it was all about two Chinamen, and one fell down and the other left him and jumped onto a train and the other tried to catch him up—funny show.

DICK: Couldn't go yesterday—it was Sunday.

JOAN: I've got an American dollar here. Daddy brought it back with him. It's got a buffalo on it. May I take it around?

DICK: I've got an American dollar in the bank, great big silver ones that big (gesture). I've got five.

CALVIN: Daddy's taking a trip to the coast by airplane.

SHELAGH: Why?

CALVIN: Becos.

JUNE: When I was sick Auntie gave Mummie a bracelet to give to me. Isn't it a lovely red. Can I bring it around? (i.e., show it to the others.)

PEGGY: I've got a new pair of rubbers.

PETER: Oh! I went to a show and all about a fire engine and there was a bell ringing at the fire station and a funny old man standing there got into the engine and the other man fell and then he said he was a silly ass and they talked about the crazy man and then he takes his coat off and tears it to bits and the little girl said "sure" and he called out to the other man and drives into the river and then firemen come along and the rope breaks and then cars come along and go off bang and that's the door and the horses have funny

56

little iron hats on them and then a wagon comes along and the man gets in and they say good-bye, good-bye, and the other man tries to get in and then. . . . At this point it is suggested that Peter carries on with the description of this thrilling show in recess as Form I have got to go and we must settle down to work.

COURAGE

The moon did not rise above the sullen bank of clouds. In the cold shadows of half-grown birches a pair of steely lights glared unblinkingly. The wind groaned its way through the pale, ruffled leaves, and faint, far cries of a mountain cat rose to the listening ear.

In this black wilderness of untamed creatures, devoid of cunning men, a common bond of courage spreads as an all-enveloping mantle, squeezing out the fears of even lesser things.

Atom-like insects find courage in the dusk to live and strive against the enemies a thousand times their size, that they shall keep their own atom-race existing. And yet, the larger creatures of this mystic world lead, too, courageous lives, for danger lurks in every corner, every silvery path and every gruesome shadow.

Courage is the watchword of the wilderness.

DOROTHY DONOVAN.

THE FIGHT OF THE BRAVES

Around the fire inside the cave
The Indian Chief sat still and grave,
The fight was in an hour or so,
And by his side his spear and bow.

To him another Chief came in,
And his pale face looked sad and dim,
And there the two sat in the cave,
One a coward and one so brave.
Then later, when the fight began,
The coward one ran and ran and ran.

C. ADAMSON.
Age 9.

THE GUIDE MOVEMENT AT RUPERT'S LAND

The Rangers have just completed the first year of their existence as the 9th Rangers. Before Christmas they took an Infant Welfare course and wrote an examination paper on this subject. In January they joined Mrs. Jarman's Country Dancing Class and since then they have given half of their time to this each week. All members are working hard to obtain more badges, and Miss Pearman, the Captain, has recently qualified for her warrant. There are now rumors of a sale of candy and home cooking, to which the Boarders will probably be invited.

The Guides, 9th Company, Winnipeg, have made favourable progress this year. Miss Bernice Bedson is Captain, and Miss Margaret Woodman, a former Rupert's Land girl, has recently become Lieutenant. There are four Patrols, whose leaders are K. Saunders, Bernice Patterson, Dorothy Donovan, and Vera Fryer.

There are many newcomers, almost all of whom are now working for their Second Class tests. Five girls are working for First Class, while two have already obtained that standing. Several badges have been won, while Patrol competition encourages zeal towards obtaining others. A Church parade to Holy Trinity Church, with the Rangers, Brownies and Holy Trinity Guides, was held last Autumn. Three of our Guides entered the annual skating races, although none succeeded in gaining first place. The 9th Company was fortunate in being top in its district inspection, and so took part in the flag competition held last October, but unfortunately was unable to win the flag.

The Brownie Pack. This year the Pack is composed entirely of School Brownies. We are very happy to have Mrs. Gordon Chown as our Brown Owl, and Betty Nutter, of Matriculation I Form, has just joined us as acting Tawny Owl. Some very good work has been done in preparation for First Class tests, the knitting being especially good.

Perhaps we shall enter the Action Song Game in the Musical Festival!

As a Christmas "good turn" we acted as hostesses to the Brownie Pack. Mrs. Chown kindly lent us her house for our party and we enjoyed ourselves as much as our guests!

FORMS II AND III

One day **Florance** and **Gordon** went for a walk in the **Alderwood** and they heard a **Macaw** parrot talking; this is what he said (it was **French**): "Bonjour." **Florance** and **Gordon** were startled. They dropped their **Brown Mittens**. Then they heard a **Bullock** running through the trees.

They walked a little farther and saw a sign; this is what it said: "One mile to **Campbell.**" When they came to **Campbell** there was a **Law** that no **Burgess** was allowed in **Stephen's** field. Just as they were going into the country they heard **William's son,** the paper boy, calling, "**Watson** beat **Yewdall** in boxing fight."

When the two were walking along the street they heard **Mr. Chown Atkins** talking to the **Jarman.** They were saying how hard business was.

Suddenly **Florance** said, "Why, it is time to go home." They ran home and had supper and **Gordon** said, "It has been a lovely day."

O. FRENCH.

HEAD GIRLS

As the Head Girl is always chosen by the vote of the girls and does a great deal of work for the School, it is suggested that a portrait of the Head Girl for the year shall be included in each annual Magazine.

JOCELYN BOTTERELL, Head Girl 1929-30, entered Form I at the age of seven and has been with us for over eleven years. Although she has been interested in gymnastics and games, she has devoted more time to other School activities than to these pursuits. She is keenly interested in organization and, during her term of office, has always been anxious to find out what is being done in other Schools, and then to build up a tradition which shall be particularly suited to the needs of Ruperts Land. Traditions are not built up in one year, or even in two, and future generations of Rupert's Land girls will be the only people who can estimate fairly the value of the work that Jocelyn and the other members of the School Council have done this year. We wish her the best of luck both on her trip to England and in her future career.

YE ELEVENS OF 1928-29

CLAIRE COWDRY: Claire has deserted Winnipeg for Regina, where we hear that she is studying interior decoration.

ADELE CURRY: Adele is at the University and devoting much of her spare time studying music.

ELIZABETH FRASER: Elizabeth, better known as Betty, is starting on her career at the University.

DOROTHY MCGAVIN: Dorothy is at Riverbend, where she is doing Grade XI work.

EUGENIE KUNTZ: Eugenie has been called to the business world and is doing good work at the Business College.

BETTY HULL: Betty seeks the halls of higher learning and is doing her usual steady work at the University.

BEATRICE LEES: Beatrice also has a business turn of mind, and between her busy hours at Business College, spends some time back at R.L.C. practising basketball on the Old Girls' Team.

MARION MCLEOD: Marion is at Riverbend doing Grade XII work and keeping up her music.

ISOBEL MCMILLAN: Isobel is also studying at the University while boarding at Rupert's Land, and is another member of the Old Girls' Team.

HELEN MAJOR: Helen is studying music at home, and has brought honour to the School by winning with her Guide Company the Division Flag for efficiency and a good Guide spirit.

ENID LITTLEPROUD: Enid is doing her usual good work at University and still belongs to the hatless brigade.

AGNES NIVEN: Agnes has won distinction at the Business College and promises to be another of Winnipeg's successful business women.

ALICE POOLE: Alice, as of old, has ambled through her exams at University with ease, and maintains her connections with Rupert's Land by boarding there.

HELEN SKINNER: Helen is going to school in Paris and is studying music there.

DOROTHY WELCH: Dorothy is living in Boissevain and visited the Boarders one Sunday during the year.

MARJORY SPENCE: Marjory, after carrying off all available prizes at Rupert's Land, is winning laurels for herself at the University.

CLARICE WHITTEKER: Clarice is doing first year work at the University, where her singing was well used in the play produced by the Glee Club.

MURIEL WRIGHT: Muriel, our sedate Head Girl of 1928-29, has become a banker, and says she likes it. Who wouldn't? We all see Muriel when she comes to play on the Old Girls' Team.

AUDREY GARLAND: Audrey, taking special subjects at Rupert's Land, is specializing in Gymnastics, and an active member of the First Team.

MARY WHITLEY: Mary, also taking special subjects at Rupert's Land, spends much time at gym and basketball.

RUTH WELLS: Ruth is at Rupert's Land doing Grade XII work and studying Music and Art.

LOWA TRAYNOR: Lowa, taking Grade XII work, is back at Rupert's Land, unable to resist the charms of the "new school."

ROSEMARY MARTIN: Upholding the honour of Rupert's Land College at Havergal College, Toronto.

R. W.

OLD GIRLS' NEWS

Births

Mr. and Mrs. John A. Robarts (Audrey Fitzgerald), a son.
Mr. and Mrs. Noel Finkelstein (Ruth Irving), a son.
Mr. and Mrs. John Stephenson (Cecily Dennison), a son.
Mr. and Mrs. Walker (Margaret Lang), a daughter.
Mr. and Mrs. Gordon Fraser (Helen Lethbridge), a son.
Mr. and Mrs. Warwick Chipman (Mary Aikins), a son.

Weddings

Iris Hayes to Mr. Edward Gardner.
Molly Crook to Mr. James Shaw (Vancouver).
Kathryn Mackenzie to Mr. John Douglas Logan.
Cecily Dennison to Mr. John Stephenson.
Marjorie Bradburn to Mr. Charles Spencer.
Martha Anderson to Mr. Russell Gage.
Isobel Lewis to Mr. Stuart Macdonald.
Beth Osborne to Mr. Miles Tomalin.   (Living at Surrey, England.)
Audrey Pickles to Mr. Keith McBeth.
Edith Hardie to Mr. H. Stovel.

Engagements

Lyle Hull to Mr. Peter Barnes.
Isobel Arundel to Mr. Keith Christie.
Frances Chaffey to Mr. Sommerville Doupe.
Madeline Thomas to Rev. Ivor Norris.
Gladys Pennock to Mr. Rodney Johnson (Toronto).
Margaret Grundy to Mr. Noel Fowler.

In Training

General Hospital.— Aldyth Holden, Dorothy Westgate, Cecilia Campbell and Margaret Grundy.

Children's Hospital.—Lily Craig and Peggy Jenkins, who graduate this year.

Margaret Carey, Beth Simpson and Gwen Detchon are in training at Royal Victoria Hospital, Montreal.

Betty Moss, Frances Chaffey and Jean Machray are on the Winnipeg General Hospital staff, and many others, including Charlotte Counsell, are doing private nursing.

Gwendolyn Jones is training in the Victoria General Hospital.

Working in various Winnipeg offices are Violet Parker, Becky Bower, Helen Read, Isabella Magill and Janet McFetridge.

Peggy Holden is taking the Physical Training Course at McGill University.

Among those doing secretarial work are Joan Bonnycastle in Montreal and Nan Billings in Cincinnati. Nancy Mermagen has been doing interesting work at the University here, multigraphing the professors' notes. Audrey Fisher has left the bank and has started secretarial work in the Hudson's Bay head office.

Those enjoying winter holiday trips include Louise Ashdown on the Mediterranean cruise, Grace Langlois Ashdown in Florida, and Enid Rogers in Bermuda. Constance Milroy Murphy and Embree McBride are in Honolulu.

Janet Clarke and Lorraine Code are graduating from the University of Manitoba this year. Betty Gardiner, Winnie Loader, Molly McClure, Barbara Paterson and M. Thompson are taking the University course. Betty Love is the only R.L.C. girl studying Medicine. Margaret Shepley is at the University of Saskatchewan. Nancy Milton and Gwen Gardner are at the Agricultural College.

Clarice Whitteker took part in the Glee Club's performance of "Patience" and Lorraine Code in "R.U.R.," the University play.

Many are doing Girl Guide and Junior League work. Marjory Glassco has been made a Commissioner in the Girl Guides.

The Junior League play, "Alice in Wonderland," has many Alums in the cast, including Beck Dennistoun as Alice; also Margaret Black, Marjory Glassco, Elizabeth Hamilton, Frances Douglas, Gladys Phinney Frew, Joyce Blackwood, Charlotte Counsell, Kathryn Mackenzie Logan, Geraldine Taylor, Katherine Taylor and Peggy Ormond. Ellen Code produced the play and Mrs. Harry Ashdown was property manager.

Rhea Roland is back in Winnipeg and doing interesting work in the personal shopping at the Hudson's Bay Company.

Margaret Matheson is in a bank in Toronto and studying Art at nights. Norah Matheson is principal of St. Mary's College, Faribault, Minn. Minerva Porter is gym mistress there.

Mary Cussans is in charge of the gymnastic work at the Daniel McIntyre School in Winnipeg. Norah Moorhead returns this year from Liverpool University.

Mary Duncan has been studying Music all winter in New York.

Barbara Pentland, Naomi Clark and Eleanor Echlin are at school in France.

Mary, Marget, Rosamund and Barbara Northwood, who have spent the past year abroad, are expected home soon.

Idell Robinson is organizing tours of unusual interest and is taking one herself, sailing from Montreal on the Montrose on July 17th. This trip includes Belgium, Germany, Austria, Hungary and Czecho-Slovakia, with Oberammergau as one of the special features.

Many Old Girls are working in banks here. These include Madeline Thomas, Helen Grundy, Helen Scott, Agnes Wakeman, Betty Holden, Peggy Collinson, Aileen Dawson and Mary Moorhead.

Geraldine Wood has been given the position of Stylist with the T. Eaton Co.

Frances Douglas is working in the advertising department of the T. Eaton Co.

Gladys Pritchard is working in the Red Cross.

Edith Hartshorne Moffat spent last summer in Winnipeg with her four splendid boys, returning in the Fall to her home in Montreal.

Maude Matheson Trenholm is teaching in New York.

Marie Weis Locke is now living in Vancouver.

Madeline Christie Dacis is in England with her two girls, who are at school there.

Katherine Taylor will spend the Summer months working in a linen and lingerie specialty shop at Jasper Park Lodge.

Joan Glassco will spend the Summer abroad with the English Summer School, and Violet Parker will also visit in England this Summer.

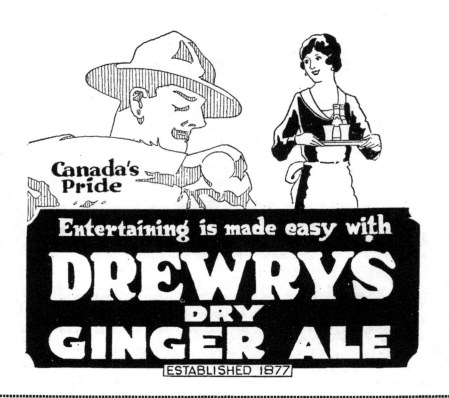

Canada's Pride

Entertaining is made easy with

DREWRYS
DRY
GINGER ALE

ESTABLISHED 1877

Pupils and Friends are respectfully requested to patronize our Advertisers

PIONEERS IN
HYDRO DEVELOPMENT

¶ Millions of dollars have been saved to citizens for light and power bills by reason of the fact that Winnipeg Electric Company pioneered and proved the feasibility of hydro power development at Pinawa on the Winnipeg River in 1906. Since then the market for power has grown enormously. Improved machinery has resulted in lower production costs and this, coupled with greatly increased consumption, has led to lower rates until now Winnipeg has the cheapest hydro power on the American continent.

WINNIPEG ELECTRIC COMPANY

"Your Guarantee of Good Service"

CPSIA information can be obtained
at www.ICGtesting.com
Printed in the USA
BVHW051115250219
541084BV00011B/1089/P